MW01045847

The Dragon

Under the

Mountain

By

Holly Kerr

To Eric Leaders,

Happy ...

Holly V.

ISBN: 978-0-9949934-0-3

ACKNOWLEDGMENTS

For Kaitie, Sam and Sarah – Merry Christmas!!

This Book only came about because my kids wanted me to write a book they could read. We came up with the idea together, along with Carina and Keegan while waiting in line at Canada's Wonderland. Thanks to all five of you – this was fun to write and I hope you enjoy it as much as I did.

Thanks to Christine for being my first reader. And thanks for keeping it a secret.

Thanks to Nita and Lisa, my awesome crit partners. You guys make me a better writer.

Thanks to Don for being the last set of eyes to look at it

The Dragon

Under the Mountain

Chapter One

The attendant handed Emma the 3-D glasses and pushed the restraining bar into her lap. There was an empty seat beside her. Emma hated going on rides by herself.

Every time she came to the amusement park with an odd-numbered group of people, Emma was always the solo rider. Just because she was the oldest, why did everyone expect her to be so brave? There were four riders to a car, with each pair sitting back to back, so Emma turned around and made a face at the back of her little sister Macy's head. At least Macy and Kass were in the same car with her. It would have sucked if they went in the same car as Matt and Dash, leaving her totally alone.

Emma knew her brother Matt wouldn't have minded if he was on by himself. The Guardian was his favourite ride at Wonderland. It was part ride, part game, like an interactive video game. Along with the basic roller coaster excitement of fast speeds and stomach churning drops, the riders navigated through a 4-D medieval world. They got to show off their gaming skills by shooting computer-generated images of dangerous creatures and scary underwater monsters as they raced to the dragon's lair under the mountain.

Her brother Matt was twelve and was happy as long as he could shoot something; add in a quest pretending to be a medieval warrior on a roller coaster and he was in heaven. It was Matt and his friend Dash's favourite ride.

Every visit, Matt studied the descriptions of the characters helping with the quest more thoroughly than he studied for tests. Images of each would flash on screens while riders waited in the lineup inside the mountain for their turn. There was the Warrior, sent to defeat the Guardian and the dragon; the Wizard who was the leader of the band; the Oracle who predicted the future; the Faerie with her magical powers; and finally Archer, the small dwarf-like guide who helped riders find their way.

Emma could hear Matt and Dash loudly debating their favourite characters until the loudspeaker interrupted and gave instructions for the ride.

Arms and legs in the ride at all time. Put on the 3-D glasses. Hold the laser gun attached to the seat. Emma had been on the rides in the park enough times she could recite the instructions in her sleep.

Another voice boomed through the loudspeaker. "Park is closing. Last ride of the night!"

This was something she had never heard before. Emma felt a tight knot of apprehension in her stomach when she thought of what they were going to do after the ride was over.

"Are we still staying?" Macy said loudly from behind.

"Quiet," Kass shushed her. Kass was Dash's sister,

and thirteen like Emma. The two families were so close that, Kass often acted like Macy's older sister.

Later, they would say it was Matt who made the suggestion, but he would argue it was only because Emma and Kass had been obsessed with the Youtube video they had seen of a group of kids hiding out at some Six Flags amusement park in the States.

"Why don't we stay at Wonderland after it closes?" Matt had suggested earlier in the day as they waited in line for the *Fly* ride. One thing led to another; plans were made. "We can make a video, post it on Youtube; it'll blow up, go viral. We'll be famous."

Emma thought she knew the reasoning behind Matt's suggestion; an online video would undoubtedly impress Hailey. Even though Matt had never admitted it, Emma knew her brother well enough to know when he liked someone. He was great at talking to her

7

friends Chrissy and Delly when they hung out at the house, but when he was interested in a girl, when he thought about her more than baseball or his video games, he had a tendency to clam up and act like a dork.

A *derp*, Matt would call himself.

It was too bad he couldn't be himself around Hailey, because even with all his brotherly faults, deep down Emma thought her little brother was pretty cool.

The usual cheers began as the car slowly started and Emma felt like they were cheering her on as she debated about their plan to hide out in Wonderland. None of them could admit it was good idea, but it would be exciting and cool and fun. An adventure.

Emma thought it was time she had a few adventures.

But not having anyone to sit with was an

adventure she wasn't looking forward to. She was in the very first car; something else she didn't really enjoy. Her car was the first to climb the hill, the first to speed down it. Being the first always made that fluttery, tingling sensation in the pit of her tummy worse.

One last ride of the night. She could get through it.

The car slid outside, the track curving around the mountain slightly to climb higher before plunging back into the darkness for the descent to the bottom. Emma tucked the 3-D glasses into the collar of her shirt. Unlike her brother, shooting the images on the screens wasn't one of her strong points and the glasses only seemed to make her aim worse. Her attention was grabbed by the moon – big and bright and impossibly full. It hung low in the sky, and tempted her to reach out a hand because it seemed close enough to touch.

The darkness surrounded her as they re-entered the mountain.

And then Emma saw a set of eyes peering at her from the darkness.

It must have the brightness of the moon; her eyes playing tricks on her. The noise of the ride quieted as the car slowed to make the corner.

But then-a scraping noise, as if a shoe skidded along a path. The sound of panting, right there in the car beside her. Emma stared straight ahead, frozen into her seat because she could *swear* someone had just sat down in the empty seat next to her.

The car rounded a corner and the track dipped down. The screens before Emma came to life with the images of fish-like creature swimming towards her. Emma, like the others on the ride, held her gun ready, but the images were blurry because she wasn't wearing her glasses. Instead of shooting the fish with her lasers, she sat staring straight ahead, willing herself to glance over to see who – *what* – was beside her.

They had finished with the fish; the birds were next, the cries of the kids in the cars once again increasing in volume as they faced more images. Emma finally dared to glance out of the corner of her eye at the seat next to her. It seemed empty...

But when Emma turned her head, she cried out in surprise.

Seated next to her was a...the only thing she could think of was a dwarf. Or an elf. Matt, with all of the hours spent watching *Lord of the Rings*, would know the difference.

"What...?" she gasped.

There was enough light from the screen so Emma could see that it – *he* – was grinning at her. He was

11

tiny; shorter than even nine-year old Macy and his legs dangled over the seat. His face was cheerful with a wide, curious smile. Emma didn't think she was in danger, especially from someone wearing such a funny looking hat. She still didn't like that he had jumped into the seat with her.

"Watch out for the drop," he said, hanging on to his hat with one hand.

The ride had reached the Chamber of the Guardian, the point where riders had to hit as many of the targets as they could to deactivate the booby traps laid by the Guardian. Emma had been on the ride enough times that she knew the best spots to hit, but she still sat holding her gun, fingers frozen on the trigger, staring at the creature beside her.

"Are you supposed to be Archer?" Emma finally whispered, recognizing the character's red cloak. Matt had read the description to her like he always did, pointing out the sword the dwarf carried. Looking down, Emma saw the same sword pointing at her. She slid over as far as she could go on the molded plastic seat.

"Hang on," he said again, but Emma continued to stare at Archer, too distracted to pay attention to what was happening with the ride.

Was it a costume? Halloween was months away and she'd never seen a costume for any of the Guardian characters. It was a cool idea, not something that she would ever do, but maybe Dash... "How...?"

The image of the dragon suddenly roared, a flash of heat blasting her face and Emma let out a little scream. She clutched her seat as the car dropped several feet into pitch blackness. Her little sister screamed loudly behind her. Archer, or whoever he was, giggled softly.

"I like the drop," he said as the cars began the uphill climb to the end of the ride. "You're in my seat."

"Sorry?" a bewildered Emma told him.

"I like that side better."

"What does it matter what side you're on?"

"More spots to hide on that side. You're not supposed to see me," the creature told her, leaning closer so she could hear him over the cries of the riders behind her. "You should put your glasses on."

"I never..."

And then he was gone.

Chapter Two

When the ride was over, Matt, Dash, Macy and Kass ran down to the exit, Emma trailing behind. They checked their scores and left the mountain before Matt finally noticed how quiet Emma was.

"What's wrong with you?" he demanded.

"I–" His sister shook her blonde head. "It doesn't make sense."

"You're not making sense," Kass told her bluntly.

"Somebody sat with me on the ride," Emma said,

looking confused and a little scared.

"So?" Matt wanted to catch up with Dash but needed to know what was wrong with Emma first.

"There was an empty seat beside you when we started," Macy pointed out. The four of them had slowed down, matching Emma's steps. Except for Dash. "Dash!" Macy called to the figure who was quickly disappearing into the darkness.

"He got on part-way through." Emma shook her head again, like she couldn't believe what she was saying. "And then he just disappeared."

"So?" Matt asked again. "One of the people who worked in the ride didn't want to walk back."

"He was dressed like Archer – that's the guide's name, right? The posters at the front say that's his name. The funny hat, the red cloak...he even had a sword sticking out."

"Why would someone dress up for a ride?" Macy wanted to know.

"That's weird," Kass said.

"It was. Really weird. He said I took his seat."

"It was your seat first!"

"I guess." Emma glanced at Kass and then Matt. "Then he just disappeared. It was really weird."

"You're being weird," Kass announced. "It was just some freak. C'mon, we've got to catch up with Dash. Are we still doing this?" She looked at Emma, who shrugged. "It was just someone dressed up as an elf. It's nothing."

"Archer is a dwarf, not an elf," Macy corrected.

"Whatever. But if we're staying here, then someone has to go get Dash before he walks out of the park."

Matt looked at Emma, who was watching Macy. Neither of them loved the idea of involving their little sister but they had no choice. Their parents had planned for the five of them to spend the day at Wonderland. There was no way they could send Macy home that didn't involve countless questions from both their parents and Macy. The difficult part had been telling Macy what was going on; at nine, Matt had been convinced their little sister would be too afraid of being alone in the park.

But Macy had loved the idea. So much that she was now hopping up and down with excitement.

"Go get Dash," Emma told Matt with a sigh. "We'll meet you by the bathrooms."

Emma and Kass were both thirteen and responsible enough to watch over Macy, and Dash, who was almost eleven years old, and a bit of a handful. Matt knew their mother had promised Emma fifty dollars if they all came back in one piece.

Matt noted that her mother never specified *when* they were to come back in one piece.

Convincing two sets of parents that all five of them were getting a ride home with someone else had been a little tricky, but they managed to get their stories straight. The story was that Dawn, a camp friend of Kass and Emma's, was at the park and her parents had offered them a ride home when the park closed. Their parents had readily agreed since they going to a party and Matt suspected no one had really wanted to leave to pick them up.

The camp friend was real, but as far as Matt knew, Dawn was at home in Guelph. "I don't really like her much," Kass confessed when they first talked about who to use.

"Neither do I," Emma said.

Matt could tell Emma felt better about involving

19

Dawn in the story when they didn't like her. The rest of the plan was a little hazy, but it would work out. As long as they got home before their parents did, everything would be fine.

He chased down Dash and dragged him to the bathroom.

Matt would take credit for the idea to hide in the bathroom when the park closed, even though it had caused conflict right off the bat. What washroom would they hide in–men's or women's?

"I'm not going into no girls' bathroom!" Dash protested.

"I have to share a bathroom with Matt and he's disgusting. There's no way I'm stepping foot in someplace where lots of guys make a mess," Emma countered.

In the end, majority ruled. Three girls, two boys.

So as people, tired, hungry and happy, were streaming out of the park exits, the five of them were huddled in the two stalls in the ladies' room furthest from the door; the girls crouching on one toilet so no one could see their feet, Matt and Dash on the other.

It took some time for Dash to stop complaining. "You've got to be quiet," Matt continually hissed to him. He had found a comfortable position – toes hanging over the seat and his back flush against the side of the stall–and wondered how long they would have to stay like that. It had been a least a half hour since they got off the Guardian ride and he was already bored.

"Someone will hear you, Dash," Kass warned her brother, banging on the wall separating them.

"I can hear you texting, Emma!" Dash chortled moments after he was finally quiet.

21

"Get off your phone," Matt ordered his sister.

"Who is it?" He heard Kass whisper.

"It's *Ol*-iver," Macy sang, with perfect little sister annoyance.

"Shut it," Emma hissed.

"Someone's coming!" The fear was evident in Matt's frantic whisper. A moment later footsteps sounded in the washroom.

"All clear," a bored male voice says.

"Don't you check the stalls?" a second voice asked.

"Stalls!" Matt and Dash mouthed in unison.

"Why bother?" the first voice said. "No one ever sticks around this place. Besides, this is the ladies' room and my mother taught me to give women their privacy. I'm not going in there any farther."

Boredom forgotten, Matt and Dash grinned at each other.

"Anyway," the voice continued, "with all the weird stuff going on in the mountain, anyone would be stupid to hang around, especially after dark."

The mountain at Canada's Wonderland was the centre of the 330 acre amusement park and housed the Guardian ride.

"What's going on in the mountain?" the second guard asked. "Hang on – gotta tie my shoe." Matt strained to hear. "I haven't worked this section in a while."

"Lights. Strange lights when it should be dark, and weird noises. Pete swears he heard screaming the other night."

"Did anyone check it out?"

"I went in myself last week and it was fine. Everything as it should be. I don't understand it."

"Over-active imaginations." Matt heard the

scornful sniff in the guard's voice.

"I don't know," the first guard said slowly. "I don't know what's going in there, but I won't be going in again."

"Maybe it's kids? Hiding out in there, making trouble."

"If it is, I don't know where they're hiding. It's pretty easy to find kids in here. They're really loud, you know. And kind of stupid."

Dash stuck out his tongue.

"We're done here. Let's get going. You watch that Jays game last night?" the other voice asked, switching topics. They talked baseball as they left the washrooms.

Matt hoped the girls would know to stay put until they could be sure the guards had finished checking the washrooms. He wasn't sure if they had already been into the men's and family rooms. Standing on tiptoes on the toilet, Matt was just tall enough to glance over the dividing wall. As he peered over, he was rewarded with the soft squeak of the door of his own stall.

"Dash!" Matt hissed as he realized what Dash was doing. He reached down, trying to grab his friend, but Dash had already slipped through the door.

"Oh no," Kass groaned from her perch on the toilet on other side of the wall. She didn't need to see to know what her brother was up to. "He's going to check, isn't he?"

"Don't go!" Macy cried in a whisper.

But Dash, quick footed and surprisingly silent, was already out of the bathroom.

Dash was always so impulsive, jumping into conversations he knew nothing about, talking to

25

perfect strangers. Matt imagined him having a chat with the guards about last night Jays' game, discussing Stroman's perfect game and Donaldson hitting the cycle. It had been great to watch, and Matt would love to talk to the guards about it, especially if they were baseball fans.

Matt pictured Dash chatting easily with the guards until they finally realized that Dash shouldn't be in the park after hours. Then they would take him away in handcuffs and call his parents, who would then call *Matt's* parents, and everything would blow up in their faces.

Maybe Dash wouldn't talk; he was pretty stubborn when he wanted to be. Maybe he wouldn't give his name, or his phone number and the guards would be stuck with a silent, stubborn kid all night. Matt knew Dash would never deliberately tell on them. He wasn't the type. Plus Dash would never want to get his sister in trouble. They were pretty close.

Matt sort of considered Emma to be more than just a sister; she was his best friend, not that he would *ever* admit that. Matt knew he wasn't very cool, but having a sister for a best friend would be the kiss of death for him.

Hailey would never look at him.

Not that she did now–not much–but there was still hope. If he went to school on Monday with a good story about how they hid out in Wonderland, she just might.

Now, if only Dash wouldn't go running off...

Chapter Three

Macy waited with the girls for the guards to notice Dash, the signal that their nighttime adventure was over before it started.

Maybe this wasn't such a good idea after all.

But Macy had been so excited to stay with the others. Her best friend Jemma had spent the day with them, and she had wanted Macy to leave with her. "Abby 's sleeping over; you can, too," Jemma promised. As tempted as she was, though, Macy decided to stay with her brother and sister. They had seemed to want her to stay. It wasn't often that they wanted to do something with her. Usually Matt and Emma were content to hang out together, just the two of them, talking about things they said she wouldn't understand, only because she was younger.

She was almost ten; that would mean double digits. Dash was only a year and a half older than she was. Why was Matt happy playing with Dash but not with her?

That wasn't true. Matt often wanted to play with her when he was bored of playing video games and had nothing else to do.

Kass was being nice to her today too, taking her and Jemma on the teacups six times in a row. And she wasn't pushing Macy to leave with Jemma. None of them were. Macy had caught on that there was something planned, but they managed to keep it quiet until after they said goodbye to Jemma at the gates.

"Anyone else need a ride home?" Stan, Jemma's dad had asked when he came to pick her up, glancing at each of them in turn to check if they were fighting. Macy suspected he would be on the phone or texting their parents before he drove away, if he saw anything of concern. She pasted a smile on her face.

Macy thought it was great that all of their parents were such close friends, but it didn't make it easy to get away with things.

"Nope, we're good," Emma said blithely, her eyes wide in her attempt to appear innocent.

Macy knew it had taken a lot for Emma to lie to Stan. Even though Macy hadn't known what was going on at the time.

Macy had waited for Stan and Jemma to leave before she turned to her sister. "Who's picking us up?"

she demanded, glancing from Emma to Kass to Matt and Dash, all with matching expressions of *we're not doing anything wrong* on their face.

It was then that she knew she had made the right decision to stay with them, to forgo the sleepover. Besides, if Abby was sleeping over too, it wouldn't be as much fun because she would take Macy's place in Jemma's bed and with both of them there, the snoring would be loud.

Staying at Wonderland after it closed sounded like it would be much more fun. Until Dash ran after the guards.

Macy waited, standing on the toilet with Emma and Kass but nothing happened.

"What do we do?" Matt asked, poking his head over the wall separating the stalls.

Kass only shrugged. "He'll come back, won't he?"

Macy asked in a worried voice.

"Of course he will," Emma assured her, looking to Kass for confirmation. But before Kass could say anything, they heard the soft scuffle of a shoe. Macy froze until the door of their stall opened to reveal Dash's grinning face.

"Let's get outta here," Dash said excitedly.

Kass jumped off the toilet and out the door. "Don't do that!" she ordered her brother. "I can't believe you followed them."

"They didn't see me."

"They might have!"

Dash shook his head. "Whatever. Let's *go*..."

"Are we sure we want to do this?" Emma asked. Macy heard an odd tone in her voice, like the time when they had to tell their parents someone broke the T.V. "I can call someone to come and pick us up."

"How would we leave without someone seeing us?" Matt wanted to know without admitting he was ready to go home.

"We wouldn't make it out of the gate," Kass told him.

"Are we stuck here until the gates open in the morning?" Their plan had sounded fun to Macy until it began to get real. Having the guards so close, being alone in the park all night...

"We'll just a wait a bit until most of the people go," Matt assured her. He glanced at Emma, at Kass and finally Dash, who had a huge smile on his face. "It'll be fun."

"Let's go..." Dash tugged Matt's arm.

Emma heaved a big sigh. "Where do you want to go?"

They crept out of the washroom, certain the

guards were lying in wait for them, despite Dash telling them differently.

"I followed them," he insisted. "They went back towards the bridge, where the *Pizza Pizza* place is. No one is around here."

"There are other guards," Kass whispered loudly. "They might be around."

But Dash shook his head and threw his arms wide open. "Nobody's here. The place is *ours*! Let's get into the water park."

Even Emma agreed with that idea, wanting to get away from their close call with the guards. If they had come farther in, just a few more steps, happened to glance in the stall, push the door open to check–Macy didn't know what would have happened.

"It's really dark," Macy said worriedly, as they left the safety of the washrooms. She kept close to Kass, since Emma was back on her phone.

Kass gasped. "What's wrong with the moon?"

"There's nothing–" Dash's words cut off as he followed his sister's gaze. "What's wrong with the moon?"

"There must be a lunar eclipse," Matt told him, stopping to stare at the sky. The moon which had been full and bright before they went on the Guardian ride, was now visibly dimmer and becoming a strange cooper colour, starting on the left side. "It only happens when there's a full moon; the Earth's shadow blocks the sun's light, which usually reflects off the moon. I knew there was a full moon tonight, but I hadn't heard anything about an eclipse."

"How do you know that?" Dash demanded in amazement. "You sound like a book."

"He knows lots of stuff," Emma sighed without

looking up from her texting. "Most of it annoying."

"Are you posting about this?" Matt demands.

"Of course not. Chrissy wants to know what we're doing tonight," Emma said to Kass.

"What did you tell her?"

"Babysitting." She glanced at Macy and Dash.

"I don't need a babysitter!" Dash protested

"Well, you don't like staying at home alone!" Kass told him.

"I love being at home by myself because it means that *you're* not there!"

"Shh," Matt warned them. "There still could be guards around here."

"Let's go then, and stop arguing about the freaky moon." Dash skipped ahead. "And put your phone away!"

Dash was quiet when they started off, unsure of

the direction in the dark. There were dim lights stuck low in the ground, but they created more shadows than light. Sounds; shapes flickered in the edges of their vision. Matt swore he saw movement beside them, off the path, on the other side of the chain link fence, but when they jerked their heads to look, nothing was there.

Macy was proud that while her older brother and sister were getting freaked out, she was the only one who remained calm.

Emma kept her phone on, the screen acting like a flashlight Macy and Kass crowded around her, like moths to the outdoor light at the cottage. Macy could tell Matt wanted to as well, because he really didn't like the dark. Dash walked ahead of them, but closer than his usual twenty paces.

Macy wasn't sure if it was the cool breeze blowing

that raised the hair at the back of her neck or the feeling that *something* was out there...watching them.

Nothing was out there. Now it was Macy who was freaking out.

Chapter Four

They rounded the corner by the mountain, coming up to the *Windseeker* ride, one of Emma's favourites. The seats stopped halfway up the tower, so that a person would be too high to reach. The top of the tower was hidden in the darkness of the night.

"It's really dark out," Macy said quietly, moving close to her sister.

"It's okay," Emma tried to reassure Macy, and herself. "The eclipse will be over soon."

Ahead of them, Dash suddenly stopped. "Who's

39

there?" he loudly demanded.

"*We're* here," Kass said. Even in the dark, Emma could tell she was rolling her eyes.

"I heard something!"

"Shh," Matt said quietly. "Let's just keep walking."

"This is a bad idea," Kass muttered. Emma was so happy she hadn't been the one to say it.

"Let's go," she suggested. "It's not too late." Kass glanced at Macy, who looked at Emma with wide eyes. They were on the cusp of agreeing, when Dash suddenly gave a whoop and took off running again.

"Gotcha!"

"Dash!" Kass scolded, but her brother was already far ahead. They had no choice but to run after him.

"I think I heard something back by the mountain," Macy told Emma in a quiet voice as they hurried after him. "It was like someone was watching us."

"No one is there," Emma said firmly, trying in vain to convince herself as well as her sister.

"What about on the ride? Who was that?"

"I'm sure it was someone trying to freak me out." That had been all Emma could think about earlier while they hid in the bathroom. She hadn't been imagining things—someone *had* sat beside her during the ride. She had a conversation with him...

At least part of one.

But for her to think it was a dwarf, a character from the ride come to life? That was crazy.

"Someone was trying to play a joke on me," she told Macy. "It was probably a short kid like Dash; it was dark, I don't like going on rides by myself. It couldn't have been anything else."

"I'll go with you next time," Macy offered. "I didn't know you didn't like going by yourself."

"I never have." Emma didn't like admitting a vulnerability to her little sister, but she was touched that Macy would offer. Most of the time the two girls were at each other's throats. It was hard to share a room with a nine-year old and Macy always thought she was entitled to the same privileges as Emma got. Her bedtime was the same as Emma's – a fact that drove Emma never gave it much thought that it might not be easy for Macy to share a room with Emma either.

"Are you still talking about the guy on the ride?" Kass asked, dropping back to hear their conversation.

"Someone was just being stupid," Emma dismissed it. The last thing she wanted was for Kass to think she was scared.

"Maybe it was like an end of night thing," Kass wondered. "To scare people and make them get out of the park quicker."

"That makes sense." Emma didn't add that it was the *only* thing that made sense. "Is that Dash up ahead?"

They saw a flash of yellow–one of the tennis balls that Matt kept with him at all times–and heard the bounce of the rubber on the paved path.

Emma sighed, the image of the little person from the ride still stuck in her head. "Let's go catch up and start having some fun."

Chapter Five

They reached the bridge over the little river, which was always full of goldfish. Dash pulled out half a granola bar from his pocket and crumbled it up, dropping it into the water.

"Are chocolate chips good for fish?" Macy wanted to know.

"I don't know," Dash said, popping the last piece into his mouth. "They're eating it."

"They're just fish. They don't know any different," Kass announced.

"I hope we don't kill them," Matt said in a worried voice, but Kass laughed.

"Emma would never forgive you if you killed them!"

"Why are you killing the fish?" Emma cried, finally looking up from her phone.

"No one is killing the fish," Kass told her with a roll of her eyes at Macy.

"You need to put your phone away," Macy said.

"I thought we were going to make a video?" Emma glanced at Matt. "Isn't that what you said?"

"Why not? We can get really famous if it goes viral. Like that guy you liked on *Dancing with the Stars* did," Matt said to Macy.

"I don't like him!" she cried shrilly.

"You did, you said he had nice eyes," Emma said.

"That doesn't mean I like him!"

The weak moonlight glinted off the fins of the goldfish in the water below as they swarmed under the bridge to receive the last crumbs of granola. Matt's eyes were adjusting to the dark and he watched the fish practically swimming on top of each other, darker shapes moving in the dark water.

"Who do you like?" Kass wanted to know and Emma laughed.

"Like you've ever watched *Dancing!*"

"I think it was on when I was at your place once."

Underneath the voices, Matt heard something. A crunch...a rustle...a soft sound like a sigh...

He backed away from the railing on the bridge, convinced whatever was down on the bank of the river was moving closer.

Moving towards them.

"Can we stop talking about who Macy wanted to

dance with and *come on!*" Dash told them loudly. "Let's *go!*"

Matt thought that was a good idea and turned to them when the rustle suddenly became a flurry of sound and the soft sigh became a loud and angry honk–

As something landed on the bridge beside him.

Chapter Six

Macy had never heard Dash scream so loud, and she had heard quite a few screams from him over the years. She didn't have time to yell or even look to see what was on the bridge before Matt yanked her hand and they were running away as fast as she could.

She was proud that she could almost keep up with her brother. But neither of them could catch Dash.

"What *was* that? Where's Emma?" Macy huffed once they were far enough away, leaving Emma, Kass and the bridge behind them.

Matt finally slowed down and Macy looked behind them. There was no huge, winged, scary thing coming after them, only the running figures of their sister and Kass.

Kass was quick, despite being only a few inches taller than Macy, and quickly caught up. "What was *that*?" she gasped.

"A Canada goose – I think," Matt told her, his eyes wide open, and staring into the dark towards the bridge. "I heard it on the bank but I didn't think – I didn't think it could *fly*!"

"It's a *bird*! *Of* course it can fly!" Kass said.

"Some birds don't fly," Matt argued.

"Like chickens and penguins...and emus," Macy added in defense of her brother.

'Well, that sure wasn't an emu." They turned to watch Emma trot up to them. She never enjoyed

49

running unless it was around the bases. She was panting and laughing, her blue eyes wide like Matt's.

"Oh. My. God. I thought it was going to *eat* us–all the honking and feathers and –"

"I'm glad it was only a goose," Matt admitted. "I heard it and was going to say let's go, when all of sudden it exploded."

"Dash's yelling must have scared it," Kass said. "Where is he?"

"He took off. We couldn't catch him," Macy told her.

Kass shook her head with disgust. "Now we have to find him. He knows he can't run off. Daddy would..." She trailed off and Macy knew they were thinking the same thing.

Their fathers weren't there. They only had each other against the dark and the guards and flying geese...

Emma giggled, and when Macy glanced up at her, she knew it wasn't because she found something funny. Emma was scared.

Matt was scared too.

And even though Kass would never admit it, Macy saw the way her eyes darted around and knew she was just as frightened.

"We should find Dash," Macy said, surprising herself with how she sounded like she was charge. She thought she sounded a bit like Muma when she told them to go to bed.

Kass looked at her. "I don't like the thought of him running around here all by himself."

"I don't think I like the idea of *us* running around all by ourselves," Macy heard Emma mutter under her breath.

Emma was scared, which wasn't unheard of. Macy remembered how her big sister had yelled that time when Muma had unearthed the little mouse in the garden. They had all yelled, but it was Emma who had taken off running down the street away from the little thing, who was much more terrified than they were. Emma had almost made it down to Kass and Dash's house down the street before Muma called her back.

Emma had the same look in her eye then.

But if Emma was so scared, why wasn't Macy?

So it was Macy who took Emma's hand as they wandered along the path looking for Dash. Every once in a while Matt or Kass would call his name in a low voice, but he never answered.

Until they came to the basketball game.

Somehow in their mad run away from the goose they had missed the path to the water park. Matt and

Kass were arguing about where they were going, with Matt convinced they weren't going in the right direction. Macy hoped whatever direction they were going in, they would get there soon because she was convinced Emma was about to call off the whole night in about two minutes. Her sister was very quiet and kept a tight grip on Macy's hand.

No one took much notice of the games lining the path until a figure threw himself against the netting of the basketball game with a whoop of laughter.

"Dash!" Kass shouted at her brother, and didn't sound at all pleased to have found him.

Somehow Dash had managed to get inside the game, behind the net where the basketball hoops were. As they stood, hearts thumping with the shock of finding Dash, he began throwing balls against the net.

"We have to be quiet," Emma chided them.

"You better get out of there," Matt told Dash, with another worried look. Dash was being so loud that there was no way guards would miss them if there were any around.

Macy thought there had to be guards patrolling the park at night, like police officers riding through the neighbourhood on horseback.

It would be nice if the security guards here had horses to ride.

"Come on in," Dash urged them, hanging from the net.

"Why don't we go to that climbing game instead?" Matt suggested. "The one where you have to climb the ladder and everyone drops off into the air bag underneath."

Dash thought that was a great idea, and quickly climbed out. Macy suspected that might have been the only way they would have gotten him out before he was ready. He led the way, with Matt beside him. This time Emma and Kass stayed close behind them, Emma still holding Macy's hand.

Chapter Seven

They found the game Matt suggested, and even Emma was beginning to enjoy herself as they all took turns trying to climb the rope ladder without falling off. It was attached at both ends, with a gradual slope and almost impossible to climb unless you we upside down and hanging on for dear life. Only Kass managed it because of her years of rock climbing. Macy came close, but Emma and Matt's legs were both too long and Dash had more fun falling off onto his back, bouncing off the inflated air bag beneath the ladder.

Emma thought this was a perfect spot to film their video and she and Matt took turns with her phone. They did one on Kass' perfect climbing technique, of how high Dash could bounce, and how many times Macy fell off in her attempt to conquer the ladder.

Now Emma was beginning to have fun.

The guard in the bathroom was one thing; but that goose had almost caused her to have a heart attack when it flew into them. And then everyone had taken off, leaving her and her long but slow legs far behind.

Even Macy could run faster than her. How was that possible?

So many times Emma wanted to suggest calling their parents to come and get them, but every time the kids voices from school crowded in her head. *"Boring."* *"Stick in the mud." "You're no fun."*

And Emma knew that if she said she was calling for

a ride, there would be little argument. Maybe Dash would complain, but he often argued with Emma for the sake of arguing. Matt and Macy would follow her without fuss, and Emma had seen the frightened look in Kass' eyes when Dash had scared them and knew it wouldn't take too much to get her friend to leave.

"I'm hungry," Macy announced after Kass had made it to the end four times and the others had long given up and lounged on the air bag.

"I gave my granola bar to the fish," Dash told her. "Or else I'd give you some of that."

"I have some M&M's," Emma said after rummaging in the little bag she carried. Carefully, she gave some out to each of them, but the few candies didn't seem to make much of a difference.

"Why don't we take some of those chips?" Kass pointed at the cart barely visible on the other side of the path. "We can leave money."

"It's probably locked."

"Why would they lock them when no one's here?" Dash asked. It was a reasonable question that Emma couldn't answer.

"But if we take something, they'll be able to tell we've been here," Matt argued.

"Won't they already know?" Macy wanted to know. "Won't they see us when we try to leave?"

"I don't know," Emma admitted. "I think we can get out of here without anyone seeing us. Just wait until the park's empty and we can climb the fence somewhere. I've got enough babysitting money with me and we could get a taxi home. We'll tell them Dawn's parents left without us and we waited for them but..."

"Good idea," Kass said. "We'll hang out here for a

bit and then head home. Mom and Dad won't be home until late. We just make sure we're there before them."

Emma felt infinitely better now that they had a plan.

"What should we do now?" she asked, but Matt held up a hand.

"I hear something," he whispered.

"How did your ears get to be so good?" Emma wondered. She blinked into the darkness, saw nothing, heard nothing.

Then she heard a voice in the distance.

"Get down," Kass hissed.

Instantly, the five dropped to the stomachs on the mat, trying to flatten themselves into the cracks to be less visible from the guards coming. Emma hoped it was a guard. She couldn't imagine anyone else coming up with the same idea they had.

If there were others in the park after dark, she hoped they were having more luck than they were.

Emma held her breath as figures appeared out of the darkness. There were two of them, oblivious to the fact that only a few feet away, the five of them were lying there inside a game.

Emma recognized their uniforms when they walked by a light low in the ground.

Thank goodness they had stopped climbing. They had been making so much noise, that there wouldn't have been any way for Matt and his brand-new superhero hearing to have been able to notice them before the guards caught them. Emma tried not to breathe too loudly, in case somehow the guards shared Matt's extra sensitive hearing. She wondered if they were the same guards who had checked the washrooms.

Should she watch them or hide her face?

Would they go away?

Emma watched as they moved towards the food cart across the path, the silver metal of the sides glinting in the weak light.

"I'm hungry," one of them said. It sounded like the guard from the bathroom, but Emma couldn't tell for sure.

"Grab a snack. This one is usually left unlocked."

Emma noticed Dash gesturing and she rolled her eyes. Yes, he had been right about the cart being unlocked and now she was sure he would never let her forget it.

But if his inability to stay still got them caught, she would never let him forget it.

Either the shadow was moving further onto the moon or there weren't as many ground lights in this area, because it was becoming more difficult to see. Darker shadows seemed to swarm the cart until one of the guards turned on his flashlight.

Emma held her breath as Kass clutched her arm. It would be so easy for the guards to swipe the beam across the game and see them. There would be nowhere to hide.

But the guards were focused on helping themselves to potato chips. She could clearly hear the rip of the bag, the crunch of the chips and could practically taste the salty goodness.

Emma hadn't thought she was so hungry. But she wasn't the only one. Was that the rumble of someone's stomach?

"What was that?" one of the guards' demanded.

Emma buried her face into the mat. She couldn't watch them moving over to the game, shining the

63

flashlight and catching them lying here. But there was nothing Emma could do. She looked up to see Matt with his arm across Dash, holding him down.

Dash wanted to make a run for it. He might make it, probably the only one of them who would.

Was there some way...?

"It's the Guardian ride in the mountain," the other guard said. Now Emma was positive it was the same guard as in the washroom. She recognized the uneasiness in his voice. "I told you strange things were going on in there."

Another rumble, and Emma glanced up. Maybe this would be okay...

"There's light coming from the mountain. That ride's been closed for almost an hour." Sure enough, Emma could see bright flickers coming from the openings of the mountain, almost as if fireworks were being set off inside. And then a glow, snuffed out as quickly as it begun.

"Whoa..."

"I've never seen it so clear," the guard said, sounding like he was scared. "I've seen a flicker, like a spark before, but nothing like this. Maybe because it's so dark out."

"Wasn't this dark a couple of minutes ago." Now it was the other guard who sounded frightened.

Join the club, Emma thought to herself.

"Let's head back to base," the first guard suggested.

Forgetting to shut the snack cart, the security guards walked away, moving noticeably quicker than when they approached. Emma motioned for everyone to stay still, giving the guards lots of time to move out of earshot before they moved.

But a few minutes were too much for Dash, who

quickly began to fidget. "Let's go," he finally whispered, pulling himself to his knees. "We'll go that way. They'll never see us."

"We should wait a couple more minutes," Emma suggested. It wasn't that she wanted to remain here, lying in wait for more guards or rain or whatever the noise was in the mountain, but she needed a minute for her heart to start beating normally again.

She didn't think she'd ever been so scared.

Dash didn't have that problem. He was up and out of the climbing area before Emma could take a deep breath. "C'mon," he said. "Let's get out of here."

"Maybe we should go home," Kass suggested, following her brother, albeit a little more slowly.

"I don't think we'd be able to get out now without being caught," Matt told her. "We'll have to wait."

"We're not leaving!" Dash said eagerly. "We're

going to the mountain. They'll never find us in there."

Chapter Eight

"Wait for us this time," Kass ordered Dash as her brother quickly jumped out of the net.

"Did you see the lights?" Macy whispered as Matt followed Dash. The guards were long gone, but Macy still spoke quietly. "It's like there's thunder and lightning inside the mountain."

"It's not thunder and lightning," Dash scorned, but he didn't seem too convinced. He danced on the pavement, impatiently waiting for the others. Matt thought Macy's theory was a good one, if it was possible to have a thunderstorm inside a mountain and nowhere else.

He didn't want to think about what else it could be.

"What about fireworks?" Emma asked, slowly climbing out and then reaching back to lift Macy to the ground.

Kass followed them. "That's where they set off the fireworks, don't they? From inside of the mountain? Maybe some went off accidently."

Matt liked that idea a lot more than the thunderstorm one.

Their father loved coming to Wonderland to watch the fireworks. They were breathtaking; elaborate pyrotechnical displays set to music. It made sense if there were boxes of fireworks stored inside the mountain then there could be an accident. "Maybe someone is in the mountain setting them off?" he wondered aloud.

"Someone else is here!" Dash eagerly grabbed the idea.

Matt thought if there were others in the park with the same idea, it might make it harder not to be caught, but it would be fun to have company.

"Maybe we should go check it out." Emma sounded unsure.

"Let's get chips first," Kass decided. Macy followed her to the food cart. The security guards had left the window open, allowing them to reach to take the colourful snacks.

"Leave some money," Dash insisted as he grabbed a few bags.

"And we'll lock up afterwards," Matt said.

"What if the guards come back?" Emma worried.

"They didn't even remember to close it," Macy told her. "They won't think anything is different."

"And even if they did," Kass giggled. "Wouldn't it be funny to see them try and figure out what happened? They seemed freaked about the mountain."

"Aren't you?" Matt asked her as she crammed chips in her mouth.

Kass only shrugged, finishing the mouthful before replying. "It's fireworks. It has to be. And if the guards aren't checking it out, it's the safest place for us to be."

"Especially if it's going to rain," Macy added.

"It's not going to rain," Matt said, gazing at the clouds scudding across the sky. "It's dark because of the eclipse and it's only going to get worse." He pointed to the moon. "Look at the colour." Almost two-thirds of the moon was a reddish colour now, glowing eerily in the sky.

"That's spooky," Macy said. Matt agreed.

"Let's get inside," Dash told them, staring at the sky, his mouth full of chips.

"That's a good idea," Kass seconded.

Chapter Nine

They quickly headed for the mountain, but Dash easily beat them inside.

Then they heard the shout, and they ran.

Macy entered with Matt to find Dash swinging on the metal barriers cemented into the ground that were used to keep the line of people separated. "This is so cool," Dash exclaimed when he saw them. "We've got it all to ourselves!"

"Except for everybody that heard you yell," Matt

pointed out.

"We thought something was wrong," Kass scolded him.

"What could go wrong? We're in freaking Wonderland after hours, in the mountain when no one is around!" Macy didn't know where Dash had picked up the stick that he banged against the metal bars.

Macy climbed the stairs leading to the platform where a train of cars was parked at the start of the ride. It was strange to see the area so empty. They had been here a little over an hour ago and there had been so many people; employees manning the ride, people laughing and talking. The space had been brightly lit with a huge fan humming to keep the air moving.

Now it was quiet and still, dimly lit by only a few emergency lights.

Macy suddenly felt the hair on the back of her

neck raise again, like when they were outside earlier.

Like someone was watching them. "Dash, be quiet," Macy said softly. She stared into the darkness, giving her eyes a chance to adjust to the lack of light.

Dash ignored her and continued to play on the bars. "I mean, look at this place. It's the coolest ride! It's like we're the *characters*." He pointed to the wall, at the posters of the five central figures.

"I'm the Warrior, because he's the best," Dash insisted.

"I like the Warrior," Matt argued.

"You can be the Wizard. He's cool, too."

But Macy wasn't looking at the posters or debating the characters. She was watching the figures stepping out of the darkness of the tunnel...

Matt and Dash would have continued their debate, had Macy not managed to raise her voice. "Emma..."

One figure stepped forward and Macy could tell they weren't guards.

Emma gasped and was by her side in an instant. But Dash was quicker, jumping in front of her. "Who are you?" Dash demanded of the figures, who stood on the other side of the track, near the exit. The train of cars was the only thing that separated them.

She didn't know *what* they were. It seemed like...

Macy glanced at the posters on the wall, the pictures of the five characters. She had been on the ride numerous times; even in the dimness, the figures looked *exactly* like the characters flashed on the screen during the ride. But those weren't real; it was like a movie. Movies didn't come to life.

And neither did roller coasters.

"I could ask you the same question." The man who spoke was taller than her father and bigger through the shoulders. The weak light of the emergency lights glinted off his chest. Something shiny, like metal.

Armour.

Macy sucked in her breath.

"You're the Warrior!" Dash cried as he recognized the man. "What – how – *what...?*"

"Could someone please control him?" the Warrior said, glancing down at Dash scornfully.

"We've been trying to that for years." Emma rolled her eyes.

"What are you?" Kass demanded rudely. "You can't be real..."

The other figures stepped forward and Kass quickly took a step back. They had a wavy appearance, almost ghostlike.

Macy moved closer to Emma and Kass.

"You're computer generated," Matt said in a low

voice, speaking to the other man in the little group. "How can you be here?"

Macy recognized the Wizard as he stepped forward. He wore a pointed hat, long, midnight blue robes and clutched a staff in his hand.

"I could ask you the same question," the Wizard said. "We rarely see mortals after hours, and never children such as yourselves. Are you also on a quest?"

"A quest? No. We didn't mean to interrupt..." Emma said. Then she let out a gasp. "You!" A third figure skipped to the side of the car and peered inquisitively at them. He was short and squat, wearing a Robin Hood-like hat. "You were on the ride with me!"

"Stop!" Matt cried, thrusting an arm in front of Emma who was ready to rush forward. "We don't know who they are."

"Or what they are," Kass added, with a nervous

glance at the wall behind her.

"Allow me to explain," the Wizard said calmly. "I am Gideus. My friends," he gestured with his hands to the others. "Joar, who protects us; Pae, the magical." A tiny faerie stood a little behind Gideus, with a shy smile and gossamer wings peeking over her shoulders. "Tamris, the prophet." The Oracle stood at the back of the group, as if transfixed by something on the wall behind them, never even glancing at them. "And you've met Archer."

"Hi!" Archer nodded gravely, before breaking into a grin as Dash waved his stick at the dwarf. "We're here to rescue the dragon."

Chapter Ten

"Is there really a *dragon*?" Dash whispered, his mouth agape with horror. Then an expression of joy transfixed his face. "Cool!"

"It is pretty cool," Archer agreed with a grin that mirrored Dash's.

"I don't understand," Emma stepped forward, pushing Matt's arm away. "Why are you here? *How* are you here? We stayed in the park after everyone left. It was just meant to be a prank, something we could make a video about and get a couple hundred likes, but we don't mean any harm."

"I do not understand what you try to say," Joar, the Warrior said in a rumbling voice. Emma had never seen a bigger man. He was even bigger than Allison's father, who used to play football.

"I say, we go now, and leave you on your mission," Emma told him, grabbing Macy's hand and backing away.

"Quest," Gideus corrected. "Not mission."

"Whatever," Kass said, stepping back along with Emma. Both of them were blocking Macy now. "Have fun."

"No way!" Dash exclaimed, jumping with excitement. "We're not leaving! We're totally finding this dragon! My dad would think it was so cool!"

"It's a *dragon*, Dash," Kass said scornfully. "How cool would it be if it burned off all your hair?"

"There's not really a dragon, is there?" Macy said, sidling up to Matt.

"Real dragons don't exist," Matt assured her. "We have a bearded dragon, but that's not a *real* dragon, whatever Mom says. I guess there are Komodo dragons; they're the biggest in the world, but–"

"Dragons do exist," Gideus said in his deep voice, stepping closer. His medieval robes looked out of place alongside the cars for an amusement ride. "At least they do in our world. The dragon came through a portal from another world – the same portal we came through."

"Oh." Emma couldn't think of anything else to say. "Well. I think it would be a good idea to just leave you to your dragon, then." This was getting too strange. First this Archer person got on the ride with her, and then he was *here* in the mountain, with others dressed as funny as he was, and talking about dragons...

"What portal?" Matt wanted to know and Emma groaned. They had lost Dash to the idea of a dragon and now Matt wanted to know about some portal? Emma needed to grab everyone and run. She didn't care if she got caught at the gates anymore. They needed to go home.

"A portal to our kingdom," Gideus was telling them. "We were kidnapped by evil overlords and taken to this world."

"You're a wizard. How could someone kidnap *you*?" Kass asked.

Gideus smiled at Kass. "Black magic. And very strong duct tape."

"Gideus is attempting to get us back home," Joar explained. "He believes he has found a way."

"When the light of the full moon vanishes from the

sky…" crooned Tamris, the Oracle, startling them with her raspy voice, so different from her ethereal appearance.

"The lunar eclipse!" Matt cried.

"We are leaving tonight," Gideus nodded his head. "But first we must contain the dragon. He must return with us."

"You want to take a dragon back with you?" Kass asked with disbelief.

"Do you want us to leave him here?" Pae, the faerie countered in a squeaky voice.

"No, not really." Macy laughed nervously.

"Without Joar to control him, the dragon would soon escape into your world. Once he leaves this mountain, he would become unstoppable by anyone or anything in your world," Gideus continued. "We have to get him to the portal I will be opening. There isn't much time."

"We'll help you," Dash insisted, stepping forward into the car.

"Dash," Emma hissed. "This isn't a game."

"Of course not; it's a *dragon*. We have to help them so they can go home."

Macy glanced at her sister. "They would help us."

"You want to go into the mountain, where there is a *dragon*, and follow people that aren't real but somehow are..." Emma trailed off, the words sounding even stranger when they came out of her mouth. "*Not a good idea.*"

"I'm with you," Kass agreed.

"We have to help them." Matt said. "C'mon. It won't take long. There's not that much time left in the eclipse."

"But a *dragon...*" Emma whispered. It had taken her

a while to get used to Matt's pet bearded dragon; this was a *real* one, whatever a real dragon looked like.

Emma suspected it would be very big.

She glanced at Kass, who looked like she was ready to head for the gate as quickly as Emma was, and then at Macy, who had a very unlike-Macy expression on her face.

"We have to help," her little sister told her.

Emma sighed.

But it was Dash, who made the decision for them.

"Hey!" Dash exclaimed, looking over Joar's sword. "Cool."

"I've got one too," Archer told him, pulling out a short rapier, the same blade Emma remembered from sitting beside him on the ride. He stepped forward into the car with Dash so the two faced each other, identical grins on their faces. Dash was only a few inches taller than Archer.

"Cool." Dash held up his stick that he picked up outside.

"Put that away," Emma began. Things never ended well when Dash began swinging sticks.

Dash clashed his stick against Archer's sword.

Instantly, there was a crash of lights from the sword and a sound like a sonic boom.

Emma fell to the ground.

Chapter Eleven

The noise had knocked everyone down. Matt scrambled to his feet.

"Archer!" Joar thundered, stumbling as he got to his feet. He held his sword limply in his hand and leaned against the wall.

"Are you okay?" Matt asked Macy, taking her hand and pulling her to her feet.

"What happened?"

"What *was* that?" Kass demanded. "Dash, what did you *do*?"

But it was Archer who answered. "I hit his stick with my sword...I didn't mean anything!"

It wasn't a good thing when a wizard groaned with dismay. Matt made a motion to help Gideus to his feet, but the wizard shook off his hand. "Archer has made a connection with this world," Gideus told them, speaking slowly. "That is not allowed."

"What does that mean?" Emma demanded.

Matt stared at Archer, who had scrambled to his feet and backed out of the car like it was hot to the touch. The little dwarf looked like he was about to get in a lot of trouble.

"Making connections with mortals in this world could sever our ties to *our* world," Gideus said heavily. "Touch, simple friendship...caring for someone here. This may result in our not being able to return to our world."

"Archer and Dash..." Kass glared at her brother. Matt wondered why Dash hadn't said anything. He had been thrown to his feet with the rest of them when the swords clashed together but now sat quietly on the floor of the car."

"I don't understand," Gideus said. "Archer has been closer to mortals than any of us, and nothing like this has happened before." He stared at Archer with his hand raised, almost like he was trying a Jedi mind trick. Nothing happened. Gideus lowered his hand and glanced sadly at the faerie, who looked stricken. "I seem to have lost my powers. Pae?"

When the faerie held up her fingers, sparks like a dying sparkler, shoot from them.

"You can make sparks?" Macy marveled, staring in awe at the little faerie.

"I used to be able to," Pae told her . A single tear

dribbled out of her eye. Pae looked exactly like what Matt would have imagined a fairy to look like. The little creature was smaller than Macy with a squeaky little voice, short and shaggy white blonde hair and the biggest, darkest eyes Matt had ever seen. She seemed to have a faint glow about her, weaker now since whatever had stripped their power.

What *had* happened? He and Dash had light-saber battles all the time and nothing like this ever happened to them.

"The light from the full moon will soon return to the sky." Dash spoke in a breathy rasp, his eyes still focused on a point no one else could see.

"What?" Kass cried, staring at her brother still seated on the ground. "Dash, get up. You're not making any sense."

"The eclipse!" Matt cried. "It's thought to have

magical powers. Do you think it had something to do with this? When the swords hit–"

"It was a *stick*," Kass corrected.

"They connected. Maybe it's a total eclipse now." Matt was ready to run outside to check, but something held him there. He felt a sudden urge to protect the others. Standing straighter, Matt felt stronger, braver than he ever had before.

What was going on?

"We must hurry," Joar the Warrior said. He still looked dazed.

"I have no power," Gideus reminded him. "I hope I will still be able to summon the portal to open, but I doubt I will have enough strength to restrain the dragon."

"You kinda can't leave him here," Emma said.

"I thought the Warrior defeated the dragon," Matt

pointed out.

"It is easier with my power to help. And Pae's."

"So you need to go and do the portal," Kass said, sounding very authoritative. Very in charge.

Very unlike her.

"Wave your wand at it or whatever. Get it open. While you're doing that, we'll go get the dragon," she continued, sounding eerily like her father's no-nonsense voice.

"Kass, what are you saying?" Emma demanded, staring at her friend like she had turned into someone else.

Matt was beginning to think that was exactly what happened.

"It's the only thing to do. We have to help them," Kass insisted.

"But..." Emma trailed off, seemingly unable to

think of a reason not to help.

"We have to," Macy agreed with Kass.

"When the stars align, foes will become friends." Everyone looked to Tamris, but once again, it wasn't her who spoke the words.

"Dash?" Kass said in a wondering voice.

Dash blinked and his eyes focus on his sister staring at him. "What? What did I say?"

"You sounded like her," Macy whispered, pointing at Tamris.

Gideus closed his eyes. "It is as I feared. You have our powers."

Chapter Twelve

Macy felt strange, like there was electricity flowing through her body. But she wasn't scared by the sensation.

She was excited.

She felt powerful.

She felt needed.

"When Archer and the young one's swords connected," Gideus began, in his low, deep voice.

"It's a stick, not a sword," Kass interrupted again,

this time sounding more scornful.

"It was his weapon, and it chose him," Gideus explained. "In our world, you don't choose how to protect yourself, the weapon chooses you."

"Like in Harry Potter," Emma said. Macy whipped her head towards her sister. "What? I saw the movies. Some of them, anyway. And when we were at Disney, Matt got a wand because it *chose* him. Mom thought she *had* to buy it for him."

"So swords just fly into your hand?" Matt asked, wisely ignoring the resentment in his sister's voice. "Or maybe a crossbow? 'Cuz that would be cool."

"Something like that," Gideus said.

"But what does that have to do with you losing your powers?" Kass wondered, sounding as bewildered as Macy felt.

"It doesn't," Gideus told her. "I keep getting

interrupted."

Kass rolled her eyes.

"Let him talk," Emma ordered.

"Who says you're the boss?" Kass wanted to know.

"Do *you* want to be? Because you can. I have no idea what I'm doing, only this wizard guy tells us there's a dragon in the tower that needs to be walked."

"I think I was the one who told you about the dragon," Archer raised his hand and waved it at Emma.

"Great, thanks for clearing that up," Emma said sarcastically. "Can you tell us what's going on now?"

Gideus shook his head. "It's too long and too complicated. We're running out of time and I can feel my power draining."

"Into who?" Macy wanted to know. "One of us?"

"Yes. The five of you will have to rescue the dragon while I attempt to open the portal with Pae. You don't have much time."

"I'll go with them," Archer volunteered, with a big smile on his face as he looked at Kass and Emma. Macy frowned at the eagerness of the dwarf. Great. A girl-crazy dwarf.

"Wait a minute," Kass began, but Macy didn't wait to hear what she said. She slipped into the darkness of the tunnel.

By the time Macy had taken a dozen steps, it was too dark for her to see her hand in front of her face. How were they going to see to make it all the way down to the bottom of the mountain? Macy remembered that there were obstacles during the quest–scary looking fish and birds that dived and screamed.

How would they get through them? And then, not only to find the dragon, but lead him back upstairs?

She didn't even like big dogs. What would she do when faced with something the size a dragon?

But the questions didn't stop Macy from continuing along the tunnel. There was a path, between the tracks and the wall, the ground rough and uneven beneath her sneakers. She found she could move quickly if she kept one hand on the wall beside her, skimming her fingers along the cool stone.

The tunnel didn't seem as dark any more.

"Macy!" She turned when she heard her brother's voice shouting down the tunnel. "Where are you?"

"Here!" But Macy's voice was lost in the darkness, in the noise of the others moving quickly and carelessly towards her.

"What was she thinking?" Macy could tell from the irritated sound of her voice Emma was angry. It made her sound like their mother. "How are we supposed to find her? It's pitch black–"

"I'm here," Macy called again, louder this time. She turned as Emma stumbled around the last corner, Matt and Kass right behind her.

"I know," Emma said, sounding amazed to see Macy, rather than an older sister about to give her trouble. "What...?"

"Macy – what's *wrong* with you?" Matt gasped. He always said that to her when he wanted to get her into trouble, but never before had his voice sounded like *that*.

Like he was afraid of her.

"What did I do?" she gasped.

"You tell us," Emma said. "Look at yourself."

Macy looked down, noticing for the first time why the tunnel was growing lighter.

She was *glowing*.

Glowing like a light bulb. Macy drew in her breath, ready to scream but Kass stepped forward and touched her arm.

"You're not hot. You must have gotten one of their powers. I wonder..." Kass said before Archer interrupted her. Macy noticed he was leading Dash, several feet behind the others.

"It's Pae. She lights up like that," Archer explained.

Macy raised her hand wonderingly and snapped her fingers. Sparks flew out of the tips. "This is freaky," she said in a wavery voice.

"But helpful," Kass added. "Now, we can see where we're going. Let's go."

Macy pointed to Matt's hand. "Where did you get that?" Her brother was holding a sword that glinted silver in the weak light.

"Joar gave it to me. I guess this means I'm the

Warrior." He smiled and held up the blade.

"Just like you always wanted," Macy said.

"Actually, it was Dash..." They both looked at Dash, standing still and quiet, gazing off into the distance with a small smile on his face.

"At least he looks happy." Macy shrugged.

"But weird," Emma added with a laugh.

"He's going to hate it when he wakes up and finds out he missed everything," Kass said.

"We have to take him with us," Matt told her.

"It's your turn to babysit," Kass said to him, turning to the darkness of the tunnel again. "We don't have a lot of time. Lead on, Emma."

Macy turned from her hands to glance at her sister. "Emma?"

"I'm the new Archer," she said grimly.

Chapter Thirteen

"How did that happen?" Macy asked Emma as they continued along the tunnel which was lit by Macy's body. It was going to take a little while for Emma to get used to seeing her sister lit up like some giant Christmas light bulb, but she had to admit it was easier going with the light. When she realized her little sister had vanished, Emma had gone running down the tunnel and tripped several times causing Matt to fall on her once. Neither one of them wanted to go home to tell their parents Macy had disappeared.

Luckily, they found her quickly, but now her sister glowed like a *Christmas tree*! What would their parents say about it? Her father would freak. Could they fix her? Would Macy want to be fixed? Would she stay like this, like some superhero on that *Supergirl* show she watched?

Mom liked superheroes; she was sure their mother wouldn't have a problem if Macy turned into one.

What about Emma? Did she have any powers? Gideus decided that she would be the guide, but she didn't know why. What was it about her that made him look at her, among all the others, and tell her *she* would be the guide? Why not Matt? Why did he get the Warrior's sword? Why couldn't she have gotten that, and Matt be the new Archer? Or Kass? It should be Dash, but he seemed to have morphed into the

Oracle, which was the last person Emma thought he'd take the powers of.

Did they have any choice?

They could have decided not to hide out in Wonderland for the night – that was the choice they all had made. And that decision had led them here. It was their fault that Gideus and the others had lost their power. Well, maybe Dash was at fault a little more than the others. Him and the eclipse.

There was no point blaming others, Emma decided. They had to help Gideus and the other to get home and if she needed to step up and guide them to the bottom of the mountain, to where a *dragon* was waiting for them, then she would do it.

Emma liked her brother's pet bearded dragon but the possibility of a real one was very different story.

She was glad Archer had come along with them

even though he wouldn't stop staring at her. It was kind of creepy the way he kept grinning at her. She had to admit, Archer *was* cute, so it was flattering in a kind of creepy way.

But Emma was glad he was here. She might have taken on the role of the guide, but she had no idea where she was going.

Ignoring Macy's question about how she became the new Archer, Emma turned to Archer instead. "So where are we going?"

Archer pointed down the tunnel. "It's not far, at least until the first shortcut."

"You say that like it's a bad thing. I thought a short cut was supposed to be a good thing," Kass said, staring pointedly at Archer.

"It can be, sometimes..."

Emma jerked Kass' arm so she would follow her.

"C'mon, we'll worry about it when we get there."

Because if Emma had known what to expect and had stopped to worry about it, they would have stayed right there in the tunnel for the rest of the night and Archer and the others would never get back home.

The followed the glowing Macy. A few minutes of hurried walking led the group to a bend in the path. The track was above their heads by now, and Emma couldn't stop herself from glancing up. The ride seemed a lot more enjoyable when she wasn't looking at it from this angle.

She doubted she'd ever be persuaded to get on the Guardian ride again.

"What's going to happen to the ride?" she asked Archer as Macy stopped before a metal door cut into the floor. Beside the door was a rickety old ladder attached to the wall.

"Maybe we should talk about that later," Archer said nervously. "We're at the short cut now."

"This is the same path we've been on the whole time," Kass told him.

"Yes, but the long way means we'd have to go up there." Archer pointed to the tracks above. "We'd have to crawl along those."

"Good decision to take the short cut." Matt nodded.

"Is it?" Archer asked. "Because there's a couple of things that you have to do first."

"That doesn't sound good," Emma said.

Chapter Fourteen

"You want us to climb up *that*?" Matt demanded. He used his sword to point to the ladder attached to the wall. It felt good in his hand – comfortable, fitting perfectly in his grasp, just like his batting gloves. "I can't even see the top of it. And aren't those birds up there?"

During the real Guardian ride – the one that didn't have characters coming to life – the purpose was to shoot as many of the flying, cawing creatures as possible. Matt supposed they were birds but they looked more like bats with a hard, turtle-like shell. Hours of playing video games had given him a lot of practice for shooting them, but that was when they were computer generated. "Are they real in the ride?"

"No," Archer shook his head. "I don't understand the magic you use."

"We don't have magic," Macy told him.

"So says the girl who is glowing like a light bulb," Kass said.

"MacyMagical," Dash spoke in his new, dreamy-sounding voice. Those were the first words he'd spoken since they started down the tunnel. He had been content to stand silently beside them, with a peaceful little smile on his face.

The transformation from the Dash who could never keep still, and this new ethereal Oracle Dash scared Matt more than the darkness did.

"Is he ever going to go back to the way he was?" Matt asked Archer.

"I suppose when we leave, our powers will leave with us."

"You don't sound too sure." Kass narrowed her green eyes at him. Since they got in the tunnel, Kass was acting differently as well. More forceful, like she was in charge.

Matt wondered if Kass had absorbed all the wizard's powers. So far, she hadn't made any signs that she had magic, like Macy, but then Matt wasn't sure what powers Gideus had.

"I kind of want to keep this," Macy said, watching sparks twinkle as she snapped her fingers.

"I don't think Dad would approve," Matt told her.

"Let's get on with this," Emma snapped. "What do

we have to do?"

"Someone has to go up there." Archer pointed to the ladder. "There's a nest at the top; inside the nest is a key for the door. You take away the key, and you leave this behind." He pulled out a silvery cube that glowed like Macy did.

"What's that?" Matt and Kass demanded in unison.

"It will open a portal to allow the birds to escape back to our world," he continued. "It will open at the same time as ours will."

"The birds," Kass swallowed, the noise sounding loud in the quiet tunnel. If there were birds above, Matt couldn't hear them. "Are they dangerous?"

"No. Not really. Well, they won't like you poking around in their nest," Archer told her slowly.

"How will I see up there?"

"Hey, what are you talking about?" Matt

demanded. "You're – you're the *wizard*! You're not supposed to climb any ladders."

"I'm the best one to do it," Kass snapped at him.

"She does rock-climbing," Emma reminded her brother. "I'd do it, but..."

""You said yourself, we don't have a lot of time. Macy," she turned to the younger girl and Matt recoiled in horror as he guessed what she was thinking.

"You're not taking my sister up there!" he shouted.

"I have to go," Macy said simply, already with one foot on the lowest rung. "How will Kass be able to get the key if she can't see it?"

"They'll be other tasks for you," Kass told Matt, as she followed the glowing Macy up the ladder.

Matt knew there was nothing he could say to stop them, but he felt like he needed to prevent Macy from vanishing from their sight. Maybe Emma could stop them –

"Be careful," Emma called after them. "Macy? Hang on tight. You too, Kass."

From Macy's light, Matt could see his little sister's hands gripping the sides of the ladder. They looked so tiny wrapped around the wood.

"Be careful," he echoed Emma, his voice sounded hoarse with worry.

"The landing is softer than it looks," Dash called after them.

"Whatever that means," Emma muttered.

Up and up the girls climbed, until Matt could only tell where they were from the glow of Macy. "How high up is it?" he finally asked Archer, who like the old Dash, seemed unable to keep still.

"High," Archer said with a grin.

"This isn't funny."

"No, it isn't, but you worrying about it is. There's no point. If your friend has taken on the powers of Gideus, than she is the most powerful wizard in your world."

"But Kass doesn't know how to be a wizard," Emma told him. "She doesn't even like Harry Potter."

"She has Gideus' powers so they'll be fine," Archer insisted. "He is one of the most powerful wizards in our world. At least, he was before we were taken. Actually, I think Osneus might have been more powerful. And maybe Ulore –"

"You're not helping!" Emma snapped.

"Gideus was definitely top ten. They'll be fine."

Matt could only hope Archer was right. He strained his eyes, staring upward, breathing a sigh of relief when he heard Kass' voice float down to them. "We made it to the top."

"I found the key." Matt recognized his sister's voice and breathed a sigh of relief.

He heard their voices, but not the words. And then his heart stopped when he heard Macy's scream.

"They're coming!"

"Put the portal in and climb back down," he heard Kass shout to her. The ladder creaked and groaned as it tried to bear the weight of the two girls frantically trying to escape from the birds. Matt could hear the shrill cawing, imagined the bright yellow eyes and sharp beaks and talons.

"Macy, I'm coming," he shouted, raising his sword and rushing for the ladder. But before he could take another step, there was a horrible cracking sound and another scream, far more panicked then before.

He looked up and saw them falling.

Chapter Fifteen

Macy bravely held on to her fear during the long climb up. Even with her glow, she could only see a few feet above them. The only good thing about the darkness was that she couldn't see how far they had come, even if she was tempted to look down.

Finally, they were close enough so she could see the huge nest hanging over the ladder. Macy listened carefully as Kass told her what to do; how to find handholds among the sticks that made up the home for the flying creatures and pull herself over the edge.

"Do you think they're in the nest?" Macy whispered as she readied herself to climb over the edge.

"I hope not!"

Macy followed Kass' directions and managed to scramble over the edge and dropped down. The nest was huge, lined with bit of fluff and fabric.

Was that a bone? Macy gave a squeak of fright.

"You okay?" Kass asked, peering over the side.

"Yes." Macy braced herself to look for the key. She found it in the little leather pouch and replaced it with the portal cube. "Got it."

"Let's get out of here."

Macy was climbing out when she heard the wings. And then she couldn't hear anything else.

The leathery wings came closer, sounding like she

was in the middle of a horrific wind storm. She screamed.

It had been scary when the goose flew into them on the bridge but Matt had got her away quickly. This was much worse. This was unbearable. She was in the nest, in the midst of the wings slapping her like wet towels. The cawing screams of the birds were so loud and she couldn't run away from it. She couldn't hide. Macy could only crouch as low as she could in the nest, her arms wrapped around her head to protect herself.

Through the storm of wings and shrieks of the birds, Macy heard Kass shouting, and knew she had to get out. She needed to follow her voice but it was difficult to hear anything over the noise of the wings.

Macy hoped they were wings. Her eyes were screwed shut and she had no desire to open them. But as she grabbed for the side of the nest, it felt like feathers. Long, hard feathers. She didn't want to know what the bird with those feathers looked like. The images of the birds on the ride were scary enough.

It was all Macy could do to climb over the edge of the nest. Her legs dangled over the side for a heart-stopping moment until she felt Kass grab her around the waist.

And then they were falling – plummeting down from the high perch, falling straight to the ground so far below. She screamed again, a wordless sound of pure terror.

"Think about stopping," Kass told her urgently, still gripping her around the waist, so that they were falling together. Some part of Macy's mind told her being held like that would only make her fall faster, but Kass didn't seem to be panicking. In fact she sounded rather calm.

"We're flying now, but soon we're going to have to land and I need your help. Think about stopping, Macy. You have to. Think really hard!"

Macy wanted to ask what exactly Kass meant but knew there wasn't time. Already she could hear the cries and shouts of Matt and Emma below.

'The landing is softer than it looks,' Dash had said.

So Macy pictured falling onto a soft air mattress, like the one under the ladder in the game they had played in. She pictured her and Kass gently bouncing once or twice before coming to a stop.

And that was exactly what happened.

Kass and Macy suddenly came to a stop about two feet from the hard ground. It wasn't as gentle as Macy had imagined, but they did come to a stop and they weren't smushed on the ground like she expected to be. They landed on an invisible air mattress and floated gently the last couple of feet before coming to lie on the ground.

"Macy!" Emma shrieked, pulling her away from Kass and gathering her up. And then she grabbed Kass too. "How did you do that? I thought you were dead! I thought you were dead for sure!"

Half of Macy's face was smushed against Emma's shoulder; the other half faced Kass. "I have no idea," Kass said, before she burst out laughing. "I pictured something stopping us before we hit the ground and it did. I don't know what I did."

"That was pretty cool," Dash said, in an echo of his pre-oracle personality.

"I would have pooped myself," Matt told them seriously.

"I thought I was going to," Macy admitted.

"We have to keep going." Archer tugged Emma's

arm still wrapped around Macy. "You have to put the portal in with the fish."

"The fish?" Macy looked up at her sister. "Those big, ugly fish from the ride with the teeth...?"

"They're not dangerous," Archer assured Emma. Macy was still glowing but even with her weak faerie light, it seemed as if her sister had gone whiter than her usual pale colour. "They are actually quite docile. Friendly."

"They don't look friendly," Emma said weakly.

"Trust me," Archer promised.

Emma finally released her hold on Macy and Kass but not before Macy heard her sniff of disbelief at Archer's suggestion that she trust them. "What needs to be done?" she asked. Macy could tell she wasn't happy about any of this.

"The key from the nest opens the door." Archer

pointed to the iron door in the wall. "You have to swim down to the bottom and leave the portal down there so the fish can leave when the rest of us do."

"Swim to the bottom..."

Kass glanced at Emma. "I can do it."

"You did the climb. I'll do the swim," Emma told her.

"Em's a good swimmer," Matt said, more like he was trying to convince himself than anyone else.

"I know, we took lifeguarding together," Kass reminded him.

"The water flows faster when you let go," Dash told them, using his strange, dream-like Oracle voice. Emma shook her head.

"Great. More weird words of wisdom from Dash. Can you move around a bit? It's really starting to creep me out, you being all quiet and still like that."

"I don't like it either," Kass shivered. "I really want him to start jumping around."

"He will when we're out of here," Matt said, then turned to Archer. "Won't he?"

"Let's get the door open," Archer replied instead, taking the key from Macy and fitting it in the lock. Macy had seen her parents avoid a question the same way. Was Dash going to be the Oracle forever? Was she going to glow forever?

She snapped her fingers, smiled at the sparks emitting from her finger tips. She could think of worse things.

Chapter Sixteen

When the tiny door in the floor creaked open, Emma stared down at the watery depths. "It smells," she said decisively.

"It's fish. They smell," Kass told her, trying to be helpful.

It wasn't working.

"I can't see anything in there," Emma said. She knew she was stalling, and if her mother was there, she would tell her to stop whining and just do what needed to be done. But then again, if her mother had been there, *she* would be the one getting ready to jump into the weird pool of fish in the middle of the mountain, not Emma. Mom would do that for her.

Kass' mom would be even better at swimming.

But if their mothers' were with them, they wouldn't be in this mess to begin with.

"Is there a light I could use?" Emma asked with a sigh of resignation. This was her part of the quest and there was nothing to do but jump in.

Four sets of eyes fell on Macy.

"I guess I could go, too," she said uneasily.

"You're not going," Emma sighed again. There was no way she was letting her little sister go with her. Macy was a good swimmer but Emma was sure she'd end up towing her around when the big ugly fish with the huge teeth –

Emma swallowed her fear.

"She doesn't need to," Archer told them. He took the key from the door and held it out to Macy. "Make it glow."

The expression on Macy's face spoke clearly, even though she didn't say a word. *"How the heck am I supposed to do that?"* But Macy took the old-fashioned key from Archer and closed her fist around it. "Do I just...?" Macy scrunched up her face, concentrating on *what*, Emma didn't know, but all of a sudden there was bright glow from between her fingers. "Oh! That was pretty easy."

"Macy will be right there glowing so you can see your way back," Matt told Emma.

"That would be good." Emma tried to smile at her brother but all that came out was a grimace. "I'd like to find my way back."

"Straight down to the bottom," Archer ordered, as

Emma took off her shoes and sweater. Underneath she wore a tank top with shorts. "Use the key as a light and you'll see where to leave the cube for the portal. Then right back up. The fish are friendly, I promise you."

"They don't look friendly in the ride," Kass said. "You have to shoot them to get to the dragon."

"Would you look friendly if you were being shot?" Matt asked.

"Or if you were kidnapped from your world," Macy added. She turned to Archer. "That's what happened to them, isn't it?"

"It's what happened to us all," Archer said sadly. "We just want to go home."

"You'll get home," Emma said grimly, sliding into the opening in the floor. "They could have made this door a little bigger, you know."

"Lots of room in the water." Kass grinned at her.

"You're not helping," Emma growled as she braced herself against the sides of the hole before sliding in, her legs already dangling into the water.

"You sound like Mom when you say that," Macy laughed. Emma growled at her sister this time. Then with a huge gulp of air, she sank all the way into the water.

The water was surprisingly warm, and felt thick, like she was swimming in Jell-O that wasn't quite ready to eat. Emma really wished she had her swimming goggles. She held the key tight in her fist, which didn't make swimming as easy as if she had both hands free, but it was better than not having any light at all.

Her little sister glowed. And she could make other things light up. Who would have thought? And Kass could fly; or at least stop herself and other from falling. That would come in handy for her rock climbing lessons.

Emma couldn't help but wonder if these strange powers would stay with them when they left the mountain. Or the park. How were they going to explain such things to their parents? *Don't worry, Mom and Dad. We don't need the light from the fish tank to stay on in our bedroom at night because Macy is her own nightlight!*

That explanation was going to take some work.

Emma's thoughts distracted her so that she was almost at the bottom before she realized it. And then she saw one of the fish close up.

It was very difficult to scream when you are holding your breath, but Emma managed quite well.

The fish swam straight at her, appearing out of the dark, murky water and into the small circle of light provided by the glowing key. And then there was another, and another until Emma was surrounded by them.

They're friendly, Emma reminded herself. *They're not going to hurt me.*

Nevertheless, the sight of the ugly fish caused her repeat Archer's words over and over again. The fish had a bloated body with orangish-brown scales that looked as if they were about to fall off, tiny eyes set close together and a sharp point like a thorn protruding out of its forehead. It was ugly, it was scary looking and Emma couldn't wait to get away from them.

Emma tried to stay focused, and resisted the urge to turn and swim as hard as she could to get back up to the top. A quick glance over her shoulder showed her the way out; Macy was still glowing in the opening.

One of the fish bumped his hideous head into her

arm, and Emma bit back a scream. Her eyes bulged as her throat strained to keep holding her breath. She took the portal cube from the pocket of her shorts and showed it to the fish, in case they were wondering what she was doing.

Emma was sure they were wondering. *She* was wondering what she was doing.

From the light of the key, Emma noticed she had finally made it to the bottom. Straight underneath her was a small indent in the rough lake bed. That had to be where Archer meant for her to drop the portal cube.

And so Emma dropped the silvery cube, waiting only until it floated gently to the bottom, before turned to head to the surface. Her chest ached from holding her breath and her arms and legs were becoming weak from the swimming, but Emma thought she had enough energy to make it to the top.

She had no choice.

Then she felt the nudge.

The fish hadn't left her side when she turned for the surface. In fact, they turned with her, like an escort or bodyguards. Emma glanced warily at them but she was more concerned at getting to the top than being scared of them right now.

And then she felt the nudge, in the middle of her back, at the base of her neck, on her arms and thighs. And then suddenly she was swimming much faster. The the fish were *pushing* her up, like when the dolphin had pushed her through the water when they had been in Mexico a few years ago.

The fish were taking her to the top.

At first Emma resisted the help, struggling against the snouts of the fish, afraid of the pointed thorns stabbing her. But the fish were surprisingly gentle.

Let go and the water will flow faster, OracleDash had said. He had been right so far, so Emma did her best to relax, let the fish take over and quickly her head broke the surface of the water.

"Emma!" Matt cried, hanging out the door and reaching for her. "Are you okay?"

"I – yeah. I think so." She was breathing hard, and wanted nothing more than to climb out of that water but she took a moment to duck her head back under to where the fish were huddled together, almost like they were waiting for her.

"Thank you," she tried to say, bubbles escaping from her mouth. And then she patted the one closest to her on his massive head and smiled.

Only then did she allow Matt to help her climb out. "I won't shoot at you in the game ever again," she vowed before Archer closed the door.

Chapter Seventeen

Emma stood dripping with a big grin on her face. "That was fun!"

"I'm glad you think so," Archer said, locking the iron door, "but we're running out of time."

"We have to figure out the traps in the Guardian's chamber before we can get into the dragon's lair," Matt said. He had spent the time that Emma was submerged in the water going through the ride in his head, planning out what still needed to be done before they could get the dragon and get out of there. "We have to take out the Guardian, too. He's the one who looks after the dragon. Someone has to defeat him."

There wasn't much left to do, but Matt realized Archer was right. They were running out of time.

"Let's go," Kass ordered. Like Matt, she had heard the urgency in Archer's voice.

"I don't get to dry off?" Emma wondered.

"You can if you want to stay here by yourself," Matt told her.

They hurried through the tunnel, Emma's wet, bare feet making quiet flapping sounds as they picked up speed. They started out with Archer with Macy still aglow in the lead, with Matt in his Warrior role, bringing up the rear with Dash. But now Emma was somehow in the lead with them, the water still dripping from her clothes.

Emma was full of surprises that night.

The path Archer and Emma led them through was definitely a short cut, even with the bird nest and fish tank detours. Matt had been on the Guardian ride enough times to know that track the car sped through the mountain on was a much greater distance than what they had walked.

They just might make it back in time to get the dragon to the portal before the eclipse was over.

Emma disappeared around one last corner and Matt hurried to catch up. When he did, he realized they had finally arrived at the Guardian's chamber.

"What about the guy who looks after the dragon?" Kass asked as Matt stepped next to her.

Archer averted his eyes. "He's of no importance."

"But he'll need to go back with you," Macy said. When Archer gave a sharp shake of his head, she insisted. "He has to. What will he do in our world if you leave him?"

"That's not –"

"You were going to say it's none of your concern, weren't you?" Kass drawled, an angry expression on her face. "You want the dragon, but not the Guardian?"

"He's an evil, cruel man," Archer began but Kass interrupted again.

"Maybe because he was kidnapped. Let him go home, live his own life."

"Your life won't be long for this world," said a deep voice from behind them. Matt whirled around, instinctively stepping in front of the others. But Kass was right beside him, her hands out and thrust towards the Guardian even before Matt had drawn his sword. Before anyone could say another word, the Guardian rose a few feet in the air, his legs, covered with the gold-flecked armour kicking underneath him.

Matt made a mental note never to tick off Kass if she could pick up people like that. Add lifting up people to her list of magic tricks.

"We need the dragon," Kass commanded, her voice sounding nothing like her regular tone which always seemed to be teasing or laughing. "We have no use for you but if you help us, we will allow you to go home."

Matt stared at Emma, then at Kass. "Foes become friends," Dash intoned.

Macy stepped around Matt. Even though the Chamber was lit with flaming sconces along the wall, she still glowed, even brighter than before. She snapped her fingers and tiny flames appeared.

Matt made another note not to tick off his sister.

"Let me down!" the Guardian cried, his deep voice sounding strangely high-pitched all of a sudden. "Let me down and I'll help you."

"You can help us just fine from up there," Emma decided. "Tell us how to undo the booby traps."

"You can't; you have to set them off," the Guardian insisted. "Hit the tiles on the walls and the pillars."

"But if we go into the chamber, we'll be trapped."

Matt heaved a deep breath. This was what he had been waiting for, dreading for the entire journey. He was the Warrior, this was his role – to defeat the Guardian and get to the dragon. On the ride, it was easy enough to shoot the tile, deactivating the traps. Here, in the chamber, it didn't seem so easy.

Kass had easily taken care of the Guardian though. He just had to get through the traps of the Chamber.

Matt tried not to think about what would happen when he got through the Chamber to where the dragon was waiting for him. He liked the idea of dragons, but coming face to face with a real, live, possibly fire-breathing and probably very ticked off dragon was another story.

But he was the Warrior, and this was what he was there to do. Only he wasn't really sure of what he had to do...

"Wait!" Dash cried, sounding more like himself, although he still remained motionless. With a quick flick of his wrist, he threw Matt's tennis ball at him. "It was in my pocket."

"I thought we lost this," Matt said happily, tossing the ball from hand to hand. He picked up the stick that he had stuck in his belt and handed it to Dash. "Help me. It'll go faster."

"He can't," Kass said, making a move to take the stick from his brother. "Can he?"

Dash was moving, slowly at first, like a sleepwalker, gathering small rocks from the tunnel floor. Matt watched him for a moment, and with the ball fitting snug in his hand, he took careful aim and threw it against the first tile on the wall.

"Perfect strike," Emma cried as the ball set off the first booby trap.

Chapter Eighteen

Macy watched in amazement as every one of her brother's throws landed right on the target. And once Dash seemed to shake off some of whatever was keeping him still and quiet, he began using the rocks and his stick like he was playing hockey. The two of them made short work of getting rid of the booby traps. Soon, the chamber was littered with nets and sandbags and huge balls that rolled out of the walls. But they were safe at the entrance.

"I think that's all of them," Matt announced after a

few minutes of serious throwing. Macy had never seen him pitch so well. She hoped her brother would be able to keep that power during ball games.

"Are there any more?" Kass demanded of the Guardian in a commanding voice. Macy wasn't sure if she would ever be used Kass speaking like that. "Tell us now."

"Over there; top right corner. Everyone misses it." The Guardian had barely stopped speaking when Matt's tennis ball shattered the tile and one last trap – another net – fell from the ceiling. All the traps laid by the Guardian had been sprung and now they could easily walk through the Chamber to the dragon.

They were going to rescue a dragon.

Kass lowered the Guardian to the ground and no sooner had his toes touched the floor, that he was off and running.

"Get to the top of the mountain if you want to go home," Archer called after him. Then he turned to Kass. "You can keep him if you want."

"He's going back with you," she said.

"Now what?" Macy asked.

"Now we rescue a dragon," Archer told her, still with a grin on his face.

Matt stepped forward, so brave in his Warrior role. "I'll get him."

Macy was proud of her brother, but frightened. She didn't want Matt to face a dragon alone, especially with no powers.

"I'm coming with you," she said, slipping her hand in his. "I glow, remember. Maybe he won't like that."

"Me too," Emma told him.

"We all need to help," Kass decided and as a group, they moved forward, with Archer and Dash bringing up the rear.

They headed towards the huge iron door on the far side of the room. They had almost reached it when an earth-shaking roar came from behind the door.

"Dragon," Macy squeaked.

"He smells us," Archer told them.

"I hope we smell good," Emma said in a shaky voice.

"Or maybe not so good," Kass corrected. "So he won't want to eat us."

Matt turned to look at Dash, standing still and quiet again. "Got any words of wisdom about this?"

But Dash didn't say anything, so with a shrug, Matt started forward again. Another roar slowed him down, but he kept moving towards the door, with Macy right beside him.

"Can you open the door?" he asked Kass when they

were a few feet away.

"I think so. But won't he run?"

Matt drew his sword and held it in front of him. "I'm here to stop him."

Slowly, with Kass using whatever magic she had in her, the door swung open. Matt stepped forward, with Macy right beside him, still clinging to his hand. She was glowing brighter than ever now, causing shadows to appear in the room where the dragon was.

Out of the shadows came glowing red eyes, brighter than even Macy, and fiercely angry.

Although Macy wasn't really sure what an angry dragon would look like. She had thought it would have been something she'd never have to find out.

"We're here to free you," Matt said in a loud voice. He stepped forward as the eyes came closer and Macy was proud no one backed away. The eyes came even closer, and now they could see the snout of the beast–blackish green scales with flared nostrils.

And a great many teeth.

"We need to get you to the top of the mountain and then you can go home," Matt continued, his voice sounding a little fearful at how close they were to such a beast.

Macy thought – hoped – the dragon might have been a slightly bigger version of Matt's little bearded dragon, but she was wrong. This dragon looked nothing like their pet Spyro.

This one was really scary looking. And big. Huge in fact.

But her brother was walking right up to it.

"We have to go now," he told the dragon.

"Can it understand him?" Emma asked under her breath.

"I really hope so!" Kass said nervously.

"He understands the sword," Archer told them. "This will work."

"And if it doesn't?" Emma asked.

Archer didn't answer.

The dragon's head was visible in the doorway now, its glowing eyes sunk into the scales on its face. Matt and Macy approached from the side of the mouth. Not that it would do any good if the beast decided to breathe fire, or whatever else dragons did to kill things.

But then Macy realized they weren't about to die.

"It looks sick," Macy said as she caught sight of the body of the creature. From the size of the head, Macy had expected an enormous body. It was very big, but too skinny to be healthy. And the way he laid there reminded Macy of their grandparent's dog when she was sick.

"Are you okay?" she asked, reaching out a tiny hand to the creature. "It'll be all right. We'll get you out of here." She touched the scaly skin, which was warm to the touch and smoothed her hand along the side of his nose. As she was doing this, Matt grabbed the chain dangling from the collar around the dragon's neck.

"Macy?" Emma said quietly.

"It's okay," Macy reassured her sister as well as the dragon. "We need to go now."

"Kass," Matt said. "The chain is attached to the wall. He can't go any farther."

"It's a *she*," Macy told him. She wasn't sure how she knew that, but somehow understood this was a female dragon.

Kass darted forward to where Matt held the thick chain in both hands. As she held up her hand, Macy could hear the rattle of the metal hitting the ground.

"She's loose," Matt said hoarsely, hanging on to the chain, even though Macy knew he wouldn't be able to hold on if the dragon decided to move.

But they needed her to move.

"Let's go now," Macy told the dragon, speaking slowly and carefully like she did to Nanna's dog. "It's time to go."

"We'll have to run," Archer told him, still outside the door. "We're running out of time."

"We're going to fly," Macy said, sounding confident, even though she had no idea how that was going to happen. "She'll get us to the top."

Chapter Nineteen

Somehow all six of them managed to climb onto the dragon, even though Emma expected to be fried by fire breath at any moment. But once they were on, clinging to whatever ever part of the dragon they could, with Macy tucked up close to where Emma assumed the ears would be, Emma thought that the worst was over.

She was wrong.

Flying through a mountain on a dragon's back was

the worst thing ever.

She screamed only once, when they rose into the air, but Macy had quickly snapped at her that the dragon didn't like loud noises. Emma managed to smother her screams by moaning softly and kept her eyes tightly closed as they flew through the tunnel.

If the dragon didn't like screaming, she must had been going crazy being part of the ride, Emma thought to herself.

She wasn't sure how big the dragon's wings were, or how small the tunnel was, and she kept expecting to be slammed into a wall at any moment.

In any event, it wasn't a fun trip back. But it was quick. A dragon could fly much faster than they could run. In no time, the dragon slowed and Emma opened her eyes to see Gideus waiting for them with Joar, Pae and Tamris. And as the dragon landed softly beside them, Emma's legs gave out as she slid to the ground.

"We should have made a video of that!" Matt cried.

"You made it just in time," Gideus said with a big smile. "Come, Archer. Bring the beast."

"Be nice to her," Macy begged them as she climbed off the dragon and patted her. "She's not bad – she just wants to go home."

"We all do," Joar said. "And thanks to you, we will be able to."

"The sky brightens by the light of the moon," Tamris announced suddenly.

"The eclipse must be almost over," Matt said, jumping off. He still held the chain attached to the collar, like a leash and Joar took it from him.

"You were very brave," Joar told him. "All of you. I didn't expect that sort of courage from mortals."

"Yeah, well, what else could we do?" Matt asked.

155

"We kind of got ourselves into this mess."

"What can I do to thank you?" Gideus wanted to know.

"We want to go home," Kass said in a soft voice, without any of the authority. She sounded like a scared girl, and Matt understood the feeling. Now they had succeeded in the quest and had brought the dragon – a real live dragon! – to the top of the mountain, the only thing Matt wanted was to be at home in his bed.

Being a Warrior was tiring work.

Gideus smiled at them. "You have the power to do just that," he told him. "Together. But you must be quick. Already I feel my energy surging back into me."

Macy knew it too. Already her glow was starting to fade. "We have to go now," she said to Kass, grasping her hand.

Kass nodded and held out her other hand. "Dash?"

Her brother blinked, like he was waking up from a deep sleep.

"Home?" he asked sleepily.

"Hope so," Emma said, grabbing tight to Macy. Matt joined her and clasped his other with Dash. Macy wasn't sure if they needed to be in that position for the magic to work, but it felt right.

"Good luck with everything," Emma called to the others as Macy felt a wave of energy surge through her.

"Thank you," Gideus said and there was a brilliant flash of light.

When Macy opened her eyes, they were in their backyard. Never before had she felt such relief to be home. The grass was so soft, the lilac tree had never smelled as sweet...

"Home," Dash said again, this time with relief.

"Lights are still off," Emma said, breaking the

circle. "We made it."

"Let's get home," Kass told Dash, who was staring at Matt.

"What's that?" he gasped.

Matt still had Joar's sword stuck in his belt. "Oops," he said, with a silly smile. "I hope he didn't need this."

"Maybe he can get another one when he gets home," Emma said, heading for the gate.

"It's really dark back here," Kass said as she followed Emma.

Macy snapped her fingers. Sparks flew from the tips like a sparkler. "This better?" she asked with a grin.

The End

...or is it?

ABOUT THE AUTHOR

This is the first kids' book by Holly Kerr. She usually writes adult fiction but her children asked nicely for a book they could read and she thought it might make a nice Christmas present.

Holly lives in Toronto with her husband and her kids and their pet bearded dragon, Spyro.

The Dragon Under the Mountain

OTHER BOOKS BY HOLLY KERR
(for moms and dads only – these ones aren't for kids!)

www.hollykerr.ca

53395488R00092

Made in the USA
Charleston, SC
09 March 2016